W9-BYQ-447

A Birthday Basket for Tía

by **Pat Mora**

illustrated by **Cecily Lang**

Aladdin Paperbacks

First Aladdin Paperbacks edition May 1997
Text copyright © 1992 by Pat Mora
Illustrations copyright © 1992 by Cecily Lang

Aladdin Paperbacks
An imprint of Simon & Schuster
Children's Publishing Division
1230 Avenue of the Americas
New York, NY 10020

20 19 18 17 16 15 14

The Library of Congress has cataloged the hardcover edition as follows:
Mora, Pat
A birthday basket for Tía / by Pat Mora ; illustrated by Cecily Lang. — 1st ed.
p.   cm.
Summary: With the help and interference of her cat, Chica, Cecilia prepares
a surprise gift for her great-aunt's ninetieth birthday.
ISBN 0-02-767400-2
[1. Great-aunts—Fiction.   2. Gifts—Fiction.   3. Mexican Americans—
Fiction.   4. Cats—Fiction.   5. Birthdays—Fiction.]
I. Lang, Cecily, ill.   II. Title.
PZ7.M78819Bi   1992
[E]—dc20   91-15753
ISBN-13: 978-0-689-81328-3 (Aladdin pbk.)
ISBN-10: 0-689-81328-7 (Aladdin pbk.)

In memory of my dear tía, Ygnacia Delgado,
and for all aunts and great-aunts who surprise us
with their love.

—P.M.

For Eric,
with special thanks to Uri and Paula.

—C.L.

Today is secret day. I curl my cat into my arms and say, "Ssshh, Chica. Can you keep our secret, silly cat?"

Today is special day. Today is my great-aunt's ninetieth birthday.
Ten, twenty, thirty, forty, fifty, sixty, seventy, eighty, ninety.
Ninety years old. *¡Noventa años!*

At breakfast Mamá asks, "What is today, Cecilia?" I say, "Special
day. Birthday day."

Mamá is cooking for the surprise party. I smell beans bubbling on the stove. Mamá is cutting fruit—pineapple, watermelon, mangoes. I sit in the backyard and watch Chica chase butterflies. I hear bees bzzzzz.

I draw pictures in the sand with a stick. I draw a picture of my aunt, my *Tía*. I say, "Chica, what will we give Tía?"

Chica and I walk around the front yard and the backyard looking for a good present. We walk around the house. We look in Mamá's room. We look in my closet and drawers.

I say, "Chica, shall we give her my little pots, my piggy bank, my tin fish, my dancing puppet?"

I say, "Mamá, can Chica and I use this basket?" Mamá asks, "Why, Cecilia?" "It's a surprise for the surprise party," I answer.

Chica jumps into the basket. "No," I say. "Not for you, silly cat. This is a birthday basket for Tía."

I put a book in the basket. When Tía comes to our house, she reads it to me. It's our favorite book. I sit close to her on the sofa. I smell her perfume. Sometimes Chica tries to read with us. She sits on the book. I say, "Silly cat. Books are not for sitting."

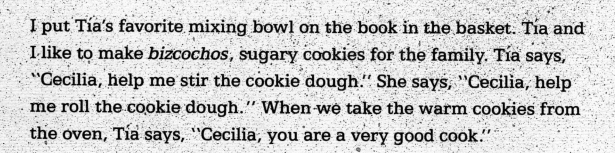

I put Tía's favorite mixing bowl on the book in the basket. Tía and
I like to make *bizcochos*, sugary cookies for the family. Tía says,
"Cecilia, help me stir the cookie dough." She says, "Cecilia, help
me roll the cookie dough." When we take the warm cookies from
the oven, Tía says, "Cecilia, you are a very good cook."

I put a flowerpot in the mixing bowl on the book in the basket. Tía and I like to grow flowers for the kitchen window. Chica likes to put her face in the flowers. "Silly cat," I say.

I put a teacup in the flowerpot that is in the mixing bowl on the book in the basket. When I'm sick, my aunt makes me hot mint tea, *hierbabuena*. She brings it to me in bed. She brings me a cookie too.

I put a red ball in the teacup that is in the flowerpot in the mixing
bowl on the book in the basket. On warm days Tía sits outside
and throws me the ball.
She says, "Cecilia, when I was a little girl in Mexico, my sisters
and I played ball. We all wore long dresses and had long braids."

Chica and I go outside. I pick flowers to decorate Tía's basket. On summer days when I am swinging high up to the sky, Tía collects flowers for my room.

Mamá calls, "Cecilia, where are you?"

Chica and I run and hide our surprise.

I say, "Mamá can you find the birthday basket for Tía?"

Mamá looks under the table. She looks in the refrigerator. She looks under my bed. She asks, "Chica, where is the birthday basket?"

Chica rubs against my closet door. Mamá and I laugh. I show her my surprise.

After my nap, Mamá and I fill a piñata with candy. We fill the living room with balloons. I hum, mmmmm, a little work song like the one Tía hums when she sets the table or makes my bed. I help Mamá set the table with flowers and tiny cakes.

"Here come the musicians," says Mamá. I open the front door. Our family and friends begin to arrive too.

I curl Chica into my arms. Then Mamá says, "Sshh, here comes Tía."

I rush to open the front door. "Tía! Tía!" I shout. She hugs me and says,

"Cecilia, *¿ qué pasa*? What is this?"

"SURPRISE!" we all shout. "*¡Feliz cumpleaños!* Happy birthday!"
The musicians begin to play their guitars and violins.

"Tía! Tía!" I say. "It's special day, birthday day! It's your ninetieth birthday surprise party!" Tía and I laugh.

I give her the birthday basket. Everyone gets close to see what's inside. Slowly Tía smells the flowers. She looks at me and smiles. Then she takes the red ball out of the teacup and the teacup out of the flowerpot.

She pretends to take a sip of tea and we all laugh.

Carefully, Tía takes the flowerpot out of the bowl and the bowl off of the book. She doesn't say a word. She just stops and looks at me. Then she takes our favorite book out of the basket.

And guess who jumps into the basket?

Chica. Everyone laughs.

Then the music starts and my aunt surprises me. She takes my hands in hers. Without her cane, she starts to dance with me.